KHAWAISH

Flairs and Glairs

Publication House

"Khawaish"

ISBN No: " 978-93-91302-39-9"
1st Edition
Language – English and Hindi

Flairs and Glairs
Publication House
Regd. Under MSME Act.

Disclaimer

This is a work of fiction and solely represent the thoughts of the corresponding authors of the articles. Our editors have tried their best to edit the content of all the authors and check the plagiarism.

All the write-ups in this book are unique and are only published in this book.

In case any plagiarism or error is found, only the author is responsible alone, and not the publisher or the Compilers.

Cover Designing and Book Formatting
Shubham Shah and Ishani Agarwal

Acknowledgement

Our primary thanks to our God. We are blessed with the energy to be able to complete this anthology.

We are also thankful towards our whole team of "Flairs and Glairs Publication".

Akanksha Sinha
I am very thankful to my parents, my brothers and sisters to always support me. Special thanks to Surbhi Di and my friends,who believe me and support me everytime.

Thankyou all the co-authors , without your support we would never be able to complete this anthology.

Co Author

Shubham Shah (Founder Flairs and Glairs)
Ishani Agarwal (Co-Founder Flairs and Glairs)
Surbhi Gupta (Project Head)

1. Akanksha Sinha (Compiler)
2. Trina Kanungo
3. Priyanka K Tiwari
4. Jaspreet Arora
5. Diya Mehta
6. R Sussannacelsia
7. Supriya U
8. Shilpasahu
9. Troyce Reimer
10. Umme Hani
11. Neer Patel

Shubham Shah

(Founder- Flairs and Glairs)

Shubham Shah, an entrepreneur at "Flairs & Glairs" a brand with dynamics in events organizing and cultural educational pan INDIA, is a 26yrs old guy who recently has entered the digital platform of imprinting emotions. He has initiated with his own open mic platform to help budding poets and aspiring writers under his brand named as "Teekhe Zasbaaat"

He is a commerce graduate from the Bhagalpur City of Bihar.

He states Writing has impersonated him since childhood and he has now been writing for over a decade!

Cooking, on the other hand, is his passion! He also mentions, trying out new things just tickles him!

When asked sir, Why SPICY EMOTIONS?

He smiled and added, "agar jasbaat teekhe na ho toh wo jasbaat kahan" Spices are all that blends! So do his words!

As a chef, he presents to you his dish! Hot and freshly served! Taste it! Feel it! Enjoy it! You can also find his writing in the Book "Teekhe Zasbaaat" and 50+ Co-authored anthologies. With his passion to explore opportunities across Platforms, he is working with keen devotion and We wish him all the very best for his future ventures.

He is Featured in the International Magazine DeMode for his upcoming solo novel.

He is Approved by Ne8x for its Lit Fest, and is a Golden Star Awards 2020 Winner.

He is a India Book of Records Holder for his Anthology Satrang, and has the Grandmaster title by Asia Book of Records, for the same.

He has also been featured in Prabhat Khabar, Dainik Jagran, and a lot of other Newspapers in Bihar for his achievements.

He has been a proud co-author to

India Book Of Records (Title- Black)

World Book Of Records (Title -15 Wonders of Poetries)

India Book Of Records (Title - Aaina)

Vajra World Records Holder (Title - Gustakhi Maaf Hai)

High Range of Records Holder (Title - Gustakhi Maaf Hai)

Indian Book of Records
(Title - Road from Worst to Best)

Share your reviews on his

INSTAGRAM
@spicy_emotions
@shubham4shah
Or via email on
shubham2shah@gmail.com

To stay tuned to his work and opportunities follow his business Handles

INSTAGRAM   FACEBOOK   YOUTUBE

@flairsandglairs
@teekhezasbaaat

WEBSITE:

https://flairsandglairs.in/
https://flairsandglairs.com/

Ishani Agarwal

(Co-Founder- Flairs and Glairs)

Ishani Agarwal hails from the City of Joy, Kolkata.

She is the co-founder of her Community "Teekhe Zasbaaat" and Flairs and Glairs Publication.

Been a Compiler for 45+ Anthologies, she is in the process for more. Co-authored in 150+ Anthologies. She is a India Book of Records Holder, a Vajra World Records Holder, a High Range of Records Holder, an OMG Book of Records Holder, a Bravo Record holder, a Forever Star Book of World Records and an Indian Book of Records Holder.

Approved by Ne8x for its Lit Fest 2020, and Literary Icon 2020. Also a Golden Star Awards Winner 2020.

She has also been awarded with India Star Republic Award 2021, a part of She Awards by Awards Arc and Winner of Nari Samman 2021 by Literoma.

She is also selected as Best Achiever of the Year by AwardsArc and Most Challenging Compiler Award by Spectrum Awards.
She got her first solo Published,a solo Compilation consisting of first 750 contents of hers, titled "Hand That Burnt While Healing".

She has been featured by the National Magazine "Taree Zameen Par" with the title 'unstoppable'.
Also featured in the International Magazine DeMode for her upcoming solo novel, she is proud to write on social issues, and is happy with the love she is receiving.
Connect with her on Instagram: @Ishani_agarwal_quotes / @compilations_so_far

SURBHI GUPTA
(PROJECT HEAD)

Surbhi Gupta, born and raised in Punjab, is currently a Law Student , B.Com honours graduate and an enthusiastic writer as well. She is also working as Project Head for Flairs And Glairs Publications. Having a Lawyer's mind and a writer's heart, her writings are sui generis, relatable, and inspiring. She has compiled 8 anthologies , Co-authored in 45+ and currently working on 3 record aiming projects. Various achievements in academics , Legal events and writing platforms are feathers in her cap. Sight and smell of her own book someday and to contribute her truest and honest potential in Law is what she aspires to achieve in Life.

You can contact her on

Instagram:@surbhi_writes

Gmail: surbhigupta855@gmail.com

AKANKSHA SINHA
(COMPILER)

Akanksha Sinha is student by profession ,writer as passion. Lives in Patna,Bihar. She is daughter of Mr. Mukesh Kumar and Mrs. Shikha Sinha. She loves to portrait feelings by her poetry and quotes,she likes travelling and capturing moments. Heart healer by birth. She is co author of 15+ anthology. She loves to feel the nature. She is passionate &ambitious for her work. Currently, she is been a co-author in several anthologies and compiler too. She has own page namely " @merelabzz " on Instagram.

एक ख्वाब

एक प्याली चाय ,
कुछ रंग भरी ख्वाब ,
चमकते हुऐ सितारे ,
और चहकते हुए तुम।

एक चम्मच चीनी ,
ढेर सारी मिठास ,
खामोश सी राते,
और मुस्कुराते हुए तुम ।

एक चुटकी नमक की ,
तकरार वाली स्वाद ,
लड़ती हुई आँखें
और मुंह बनाते हुए तुम।

एक कटोरी शिकायत की ,
तनी तनी तेरी निगाहें ,
रूठी हुई सी मुस्कान
और मनाते हुए तुम

एक मुट्ठी अधिकार का,
बगावती से लम्हे की,
झिलमिलाती हुई "हाँ "
और नज़र झुकाते हुए तुम ।

एक डली विश्वास की ,
बिखरती हुई आशंकाएं ,
महफुस से एहसास

और गर्वित से तुम

एक कतरा खुमारी का,
बेफिक्र सी हवाएं ,
सन्नाटों की गूंज
और अधजगे से तुम

एक नज़र भर शैतानी ,
हँसते हुए लम्हे ,
बेपरवाह सी मैं
और ठहाके लगाते तुम

एक इकाई का आक्रोश ,
कुछ आँखों के मोती ,
बिखेरती हुई मैं
और समेटते हुए तुम

एक बालिश्त अल्फ़ाज़ ,
सहमी हुई सी राग ,
गुनगुनाती हुई मैं
और खामोश से तुम

एक बूंद हँसी ,
बकवास सी बातें ,
सरफिरी सी मैं,
और समझदार से तुम

एक शाम की थकान ,
बहुत सारी भीड़ ,
कुछ परेशान सी मैं

और हाथ थामे तुम

एक पहर सुकून ,
भीगी हुई सड़क ,
जगमगाती पीली रोशनी
और साथ चलते हम बस ...

इतना ही तो चाहिए
एक खुबसूरत ज़िन्दगी के लिए बस
"तुम्हारा होना " चाहिए ..

<u>तेरे दिल का नजराना</u>

तेरे दिल का नजराना तू मुझको ना देना
पर तेरी सांसों की माला में मुझको रखना
तू भूले से भी याद मुझे मत करना
पर अपने एहसासों में याद मुझे रखना
तू अपने अरमानों में मुझे मत रखना
पर अपनी भूली बिसरी यादों में मुझे रखना
साँझ ढले तो तू मुझे दरवाजे पर मत तकना
पर रात घिरे तो सितारों में तू मुझे तकना
जीवन में तू मुझको कभी राहों में ना देखना
पर हर रात सपनों में मेरा दीदार तो करना
आँख खुले तो तू मुझको ना मिलना
पर हो पलकें बंद तो तू ही दिखना
समय की दौड़ में समय के साथ चलना
पर समय रुक जाये तो मेरे साथ चलना

ख़्वाहिशों

मेरे दिल की ख़्वाहिशों को बरसा जा
तू रात नींदों में मुझको जगा जा
मेरी वीरान राहों का मुसाफ़िर बनकर
मेरी मंजिल पर हाज़िरी लगा जा
मेरी टूटी हुई कश्ती पर चढ़कर
मुझको किनारे का दर्शन करा जा
बहुत पीर है मेरे दिल के भँवर में
मेरी पीर को अपनी पीर में मिला जा
बहुत रोया हूँ रातों के सफर में
जिन्दगी की खोई किरण दिखा जा
मेरी जिन्दगी की कहानी के पर्दे से
बे-रंग बेकार अल्फ़ाज़ मिटा जा
इस रंग बदलती दुनिया में मुझको
जीने का कोई सलीका सिखा जा
आज पानी और आँसू एक लगते है
फुर्सत मिले तो अंतर बता जा
हूँ गलत मैं कहीं तो जमाने में
मेरी जिन्दगी को फिर ठुकरा जा
आज मैं से बड़ा मैं का नाम हो गया
मुझको तो मेरे ही दर्शन करा जा
तू आए या ना आए किसको खबर
जहाँ से निकलकर मुझमें समा जा

तुम भी मुझे याद करो

तुम भी मुझे याद करो, ये ख्वाहिश नहीं मेरी||
तुम यू ही याद आ जाती हो, ये बसकी बात नहीं मेरी||
तुम भी मुझे इतनी शिद्दत से चाहों, ये ख्वाहिश नहीं मेरी||
मैं तुम्हें भूल जाऊ, ये बसकी बात नहीं मेरी||
अक्सर अकेला बैठा जब उन गज़लों को गुनगुनाता हू,
जो बीते दिनो की याद दिलाते हैं तुम्हारी और मेरी||

लेकिन कभी चाहत नहीं रखता की तुम भी उन्ही कूचों पे वापस
आओ, जो तुम्हें याद दिलाये मेरी||
मैं अक्सर उस कूंचे में आज भी घूम आता हू, जहाँ तुम्हें देख कर
सांसे रुक जाया करती थी मेरी||
आज चाह कर भी सांसे रोकने की कोशिश करता हू उन गलिहारों
मे, तो ये ख्वाहिश अधूरी सी रहे जाती है मेरी||
आज जानबूझ कर हर वो जुर्म करने की ख्वाहिश है मेरी||
जिससे मुलाक़ात हो जाए तुमसे, और सांसो को अलविदा कहे दे ये
धड़कन मेरी||

Trina Kanungo

Trina Kanungo, an executive officer ECGC Ltd, a government of India enterprise, posted in Mumbai, has been a student of Mathematics till her Masters, an ardent lover of Indian literature and Indian folk art, till date. Calm and composed by nature, she loves to piant nature and yearns to create an eden of poesy, in the crude canvas of life.

A Holy Yearning

Grandpa is back from Haridwar, with loads of Shiv Lingas for everyone; but nothing for her mother! "But why Maa?", Barkha asked . Megha was astouned, she had no clue, how to answer her little angel's query. Megha has no son, and that is the biggest flaw ever on her part. But what explanation was anticipated by the little girl?

Seeing her mother confused and flabbergasted, Barkha gave a moist kiss to her cheeks, "Maa, donot worry, let me grow up, I will go to Kashi and buy a nice shiv linga for you."

Megha laughed aloud, "my crazy girl, Kashi is a holy place for the grannies to visit, not for babies like you! Come on, have your milk". Megha started patting her , and tears rolled down her cheeks. This was the first time, she did not feel low of being the parent of a girl child.

It has been seventeen years now, Barkha is now posted as a government officer in the export sector, earning a descent salary. Office has deputed her with some urgent assignment in Varanasi branch, for two weeks. After completing all her assignments, she went to the mighty campus of Benaras Hindu University, which was her dream university, in her student life. She was literally enthralled with the green ambience of the campus. The next day, her colleagues arranged a trip to the Kashi Vishwanath Temple for her.

It was a cool yet sun kissed morning, with a vibrant hue and a holy redolence of the Ganges, that embraced the temple locale. Barkha was almost carried away by the composed aura of the Ganges. She felt goosebupms as she entered the temple zone. As she was about to enter the main worship

area, suddenly her eyes got stuck to a beautiful white Shiva Linga. At once she was reminded of her mother's droopy face, long ago; she smile mildly, and along with the puja thali she paid for that pious Shiva Linga too.

After returning home, she saw, Megha was busy cooking her favourite dishes. She at once hugged her, "Maa, look, what I have for you!" Megha somehow puzzled," what now? Let me finish my cooking, you are hungry by now!" But Barkha forced her to see the gift pack immediately. As Megha unpacked the wrap, the secret clouds got receded from her soul, and her eyes sparkled, it was a radiant divine Shiva Linga made of white marble stone. Today, Megha could not control her tears, it was not out of dismay, but out of sheer joy of victory!

Yes, she is the mother of a girl child, she is second to none, she is Barkha's "Maa"!

A Whimsical Desire

Do we live for food or money?
Answer to this mystery is yet unsolved.
When the rain recedes,
we long to see the fogs undissolved.
When we call for a shelter
out of mud and stone,
a place to recline,
an abode of undisturbed zone.
Sitting beside the lazy sea-shore,
as I cast around the waves,
I couldnot but find a smile
amidst the implicit dark graves.
We are ephemeral beings,
with a hunger for food and love,
and a close affinity to eternal solace
heading towards the infinite sky above.

Priyanka K. Tiwari

Priyanka had a poetic disposition right from childhood. Her first poem was published in a newspaper at the age of 8. She has written many poems in English and Hindi, some of which were published in local newspapers and magazines. For her, poetry is " Words that breathe, Emotions that bleed". A graduate in Biotechnology, she is currently associated with the field of HR- Organizational Psychology. Travelling, photography and reading are her passions. She can be contacted on Instagram at @pri_at_insta

उन्मुक्त मन की अभिलाषा

कितने सुनहले, कितने प्यारे
कितने लगते हैं लुभावने
सजे हैं सब इन पलकों में
ख्वाब कितने ही सुहावने !

ताक रहे हैं ये तृषित नैन
तारकों से भरा आसमान
उसे झुका, उच्च शिखर पर
होना है मुझे विराजमान !

दूर-दूर तक जा-जाकर
है नील गगन में घूमना।
उम्मीदों के पंख लगा कर
खूब खुशी से है झूमना !

बनकर कोई पंछी पागल
उड़ना है क्षितिज के पार ;
आए चाहे कोई रुकावट
नहीं मानना मुझको हार !

पहन कीर्ति का मुकुट
दुनिया पर है छा जाना
अजर अमर बनकर मुझे
सबसे ऊपर है जाना !

पथरीला हो रास्ता कितना
घबराना है उससे व्यर्थ
जिंदगी को समेट-संवार

देना है उसे नया अर्थ ।

ये जोश , उमंग , साहस
ले मन में अनोखा आकार
कुछ लड़ , कुछ कर, कुछ बढ़कर
करना है हर सपना साकार !

तारे सारे तोड़ने को
हो रहा मन परेशान
बेड़ियां तोड़ सारी अब
भरनी है ऊंची उड़ान !

Re-discovering Myself

I was hopelessly lost; meandering through the realms of dark,
When upon a new journey, I accidentally did embark...

That led to the discovery of my Self true;
All my limited self-conceptions, it did undo!

Erstwhile I had led a life not truly of my own,
Orchestrated by conditioning, my soul torn;

My Inner Light, eclipsed by my towering ego
Discernment clouded; couldn't tell a friend from a foe

Fragments of me, lost in gratification of senses
My inherent powers, diluted by petty indulgences

My mind, stuffed with what others fed...
Woe! Was it even my life that I led?

But today I am free, all by myself, alone,
My soul, my heart - for none but my own!

Shallow goals, my mind's long outgrown
A renewed dream, my eager heart's sown!

I have re-discovered my passions, ideals and aspirations,
Discarding my passivity, fears and self-imposed limitations!

I have a vision of my own to live by,
Let the world protest and ask why...

My potential, far exceeds what I had thoeght,
Only in my Higher Self, refuge I have sought!

Peace I have found, responding to my Higher Calling
I am defined by possibilities; not by any past failing!

To my inner Voice, I shall forever listen,
Under its aegis, I shall glow and glisten.

Faith in my Own Self, and guided by the Divine Will
I renew my soul's mission – that greater Destiny to fulfill!

जसप्रीत अरोरा

" लिखदूं कुछ ऐसा की दुनिया बदल जाए,
धुंध लूँ खुद को इन शब्दों में कहीं के लिखने की एक नयी वजह
मिल जाए। "

जसप्रीत अरोरा एक कवियत्री हैं और उनकी लिखी कुछ और
रचनाएँ पढ़ने के लिए उनका इंस्टाग्राम पेज देखिये - .incarnation.

गलत/ सही

तुम दूर बड़े ,
पर लगता है की मेरे पास खड़े।
मेरी कहानियों ने कहीं रख सा लिया है तुमको ,
मेरी कविताओं ने एक घर देदिया है हमको।
उस सूखे पुराने गुलाब के जैसे ,
समेत लिया है तुमको इन किताबों ने कहीं ,
मैं फेक दूँ ये एक फूल कैसे ?
तुम नहीं तुम्हारी यादें ही सही।
फाड़ कर फेंकू तोह कहाँ ?
इन कागज़ों की बस एक ही है जगह।
उस कोने में जहा आता जाता कोई नहीं,
उस दुनिया में जहाँ न कुछ गलत न कुछ सही।

गम नहीं।

सोचती हूँ के कुछ वक़्त के लिए तुम्हारे बारे में सोचना छोड़ दूँ।
तब याद आता है की कविताएं लिखूंगी किस पर ?
सोचती हूँ के कुछ वक़्त के लिए तुम्हारी बातें करना छोड़ दूँ।
तब याद आता है की बात करूँगी तोह किस पर ?
में भूल चुकी हूँ के ज़िन्दगी में तुम्हारे बगैर भी गुज़ारा हो सकता है ,
में भूल चुकी हूँ के प्यार दोबारा भी हो सकता है।
ख्वाइश है अब बस एक बार समझने की ,
के ज़िन्दगी में तुम नहीं तोह भी कोई गम नहीं।
रोकलु तुम्हे मेरे शब्दों में बदलने से ,
के तुम्हारे इलावा कुछ भी और लिखने के लिए इस कलम में
सियाही कम नहीं।
के ज़िन्दगी में तुम नहीं तोह भी कोई गम नहीं।

<u>रंग।</u>

मुझसे अक्सर कहा जाया करता है की मेरी लिखारी मेरी उम्र से
कई ज़्यादा बड़ी है।
मुझे अक्सर बताया जाता है की छोड़ो ये सब बातें अरे ये ज़िन्दगी
बहुत बड़ी है।
जो छूट गया उसे जाने दो ,
जो आगया उसे आने दो।
मैं मुस्कुरा कर परे हो जाय करती हूँ ,
क्युकी सिर्फ तुम पर लिखी कविताओं में मैं खुद को पाया करती हूँ।
जो छूट गया उसे जाने दूँ ?
और अपने शब्दों को अपने तक न आने दूँ ?
मुझे हमेशा कहा जाता है के ये उम्र नहीं है इन बातो की ,
बस में पूछती हूँ क्या कोई भी उम्र होती है इन हालातों की ?
मुझे कह लेने दो ,
मेरे रंगो को मेरे गीतों की धुन पर बह लेने दो।

फ़िज़ूल।

ख्वाइश है ज़रा सी , मैं आखें बंद करू और तू मिल जाए। तमन्ना है ज़रा सी , मैं पीछे मुड़ूं तोह तू दिख जाए। मैं बोलू और तू सुनले , बस ये ज़िन्दगी मुझे तेरे लिए चुन ले। मैं देखूं तुझे तोह बस तू मेरी कहानियों में न हो , जहा देखूं तुझे तू वहान हो। तू समझे मुझे बस इतनी सी आरज़ू है , के बिन तेरे जीना बिलकुल फ़िज़ूल है।

आफत।

लाख छुपाओ छुपता नहीं , ये रंग है उस प्यार का। लाख बुलाओ सुनता नहीं , ये ढंग है उस प्यार का। नशा कहो या कहो इसे आदत, मज़ा कहो या कहो इसे आफत। ये वो गीत है जो जुबां से उतरता नहीं , ये सुनता तोह बहुत कुछ है पर कुछ कहता नहीं। शब्द कम पड़ जाया करते हैं , तारीफ में इसकी। तारीफों के फूल कम पड़ जाय करते हैं , उसतत में इसकी। लाख भुलालो चाहे ये भुलाया जा सकता नहीं , ये खूबी है उस प्यार की। ये इश्क़ का मकान है यहाँ उसकी मर्ज़ी के खिलाफ कहीं जाया जा सकता नहीं, ताकत ही अनोखी है उस प्यार की।

<u>जल्दी आना।</u>

समझ आये तोह मुझे भी समझाना, ये इश्क़ का फ़साना।   कुछ पता चले तोह मुझे भी बातना, ये तेज़ बड़ा है ज़माना।   मैं कहूं क्या ऐसा जो तुम सब जानते नहीं , वो बात भी थी पता तुम्हे और मालूम है ये भी।   बस कुछ नज़र आए तोह मुझे भी दिखाना, ए ! इस बार ज़रा ठहर जाना। वो आए तोह मुझे भी बुलाना, ए ! इस बार कोई बहाना मत बनाना।   - थोड़ा जल्दी आना

शाम   समझ मेरे आता नहीं के अब क्या करू , रोज़ सुबह उठती हूँ ये सोच कर के तुम्हे याद नहीं करुँगी ज़ारा भी दिन भर आज। और तुम्हे याद करते करते शाम आजाती है।

Diya Mehta

Diya Mehta is a young author of 16 years . She is a school going girl of 11th standard. She is dedicated towards her writings since she was 13 years old. She can achieve heights by her own support and confidence.

Your wish !?

What's your wish ?
What's your dream ?
Life is a miracle ,to fulfil that wish.
You are his wish ,
You are his dream.
God is going to accomplish that,
Either knowingly or by wheam.
Let us wish to complete that wish ,
Thinking of it won't work,
Working on it may get into work.
Floating on dream,holding your wishes,
In a big shape of fate,
Is a big journey of life.
Full of hardships, full of pain,
Life will fulfil all of it.
What can be salty or can be sweet ,
But at last you reach on island corner,
Where are you would get all the wishes coming true !

Wishes to all wishes

Wishes are to all wishes ,
Life is to all wishes ,
Dreams to fulfill all wishes ,
Fate has all wishes.

Day by day , time to time ,
Wishes increase , life and fate remains the same.
Move along it all, run with it ,
Never drown down to it.

Life is a purpose ,
Dreaming a right , let's get a chance ,
To win the wishes all abright.

Jump on the life, holding a wish ,
Catching a dream, hopping a lane.
Every wish has a purpose,
Don't worry , life's working on it ,
Fate rowing through it.

Wishes

Wishes are more time is less
Life is short give it a bliss.
What you wish to have is a desire,
what you have is a wish of God.
Wait for the life to give the chance,
Fulfill the wish,
Not enhance but by what you have.
Wishes are necessary but be thankful for what you have ,
God is their , wishes come true !
God support to fulfil the wish
But by hope not by greed.
Let it be special , let it be charming.
Let's give wishes a path , rather than giving a way .

ना रह जाए दूर - ख्वाहिशें

ख्वाहिशें कही अधूरी न राह जाए , जो ज़िंदगी चले आपने इशारों पार वो मुमकिन कहाँ , जो ख़्वाहिश मुक़ाम तक ना जाए वो मंज़िल कहा । उस क़िस्मत की ख़्वाहिशों से थोड़ी है दुश्मनी , साथ दे जब क़िस्मत तो ख्वाहिशें है अधूरी , ख्वाहिशें जब साथ हो तो क़िस्मत राह बदल देती । ताज्जुब की बात यह है कि , कभी - कभी मरते दम तक ख्वाहिशें राह जाती है अधूरी, उनको पूरा करने के लिए या तो ज़िंदगी साथ नहीं देती या क़िस्मत बदल जाती है । उस बीते कल में भी है ख़्वाहिश , जो पल आने वाला है , है उसमें भी ख्वाहि

ख़्वाबों की ख़्वाहिशें

हज़ारों ख़्वाहिशें एक साथ तोली , तोलकर देखा तो भारी थी । उस पुरानी ख्वाहिश का तोल , वो ही पुरानी ज़िद , अब चाहिए हर हसीन पल उस ख्वाहिश के संग । हम सब कैदी है यहाँ , कोई ख़्वाहिशों का तो कोई ख़्वाबों का , सब ख़्वाहिशें पूरी होंगी तो मार दोगे उम्मीद , जिसके सहारे ज़िंदगी है यही । वो ख़्वाहिशें रह गयी अधूरी , वो ख़्वाब भी रह गये अधूरे , अब पूरी है तो सिर्फ़ उम्मीद , अब पूरी है तो सिर्फ़ उम्मीद ।

वो ख़्वाहिशें

उन ख्वाहिशों के ख़ातिर जी रहे है , पूरी करनी है वो ख्वाहिशें , दिल डूब जाता है उस पल में , मगर अब ठान लिया है पूरी करूँगी वो ख्वाहिशें , अपने ठेके से । कुछ ऐसी ना रह जाए ख्वाहिशें , जिसकी उम्र नही है और उम्र ना रहे । ख्वाहिश ऐसे पूरी करनी है , कि ख़्वाब और ख्वाहिश अधूरी ना रह जाए । दिल - दिमाग़ से अब कोण करना है , कही दृष्टि से निशाना ना छूट जाए । उन ख्वाहिशों के ख़ातिर जी रहे है , पूरी करनी है वो ख्वाहिशें । उस ज़हन में दिल डूब गया , हिम्मत बड़ गयीं वो ख्वाहिश पूरी करने के लिए । अब पूरी होगी मेरी वो ख्वाहिशें ।

ख्वाहिशें अधूरी

मेरी हर ख़्वाहिश लेती है मेरी उम्मीद का सहारा , मेरी हर कोशिश लेती है मेरी क़िस्मत का सहारा । वो ख्वाहिशें सहम उठी है , ना जाने क्यों ज़रूरतों ने उससे ऊँचा बोला , वो ही ख़्वाहिश संकुच सी गई है । उनको ज़िंदगी में हिस्सों में बाँट दिया है , मालूम है ख़्वाब अधूरे है , ख्वाहिशें बड़ी है , पर जनाब क्या करे ज़िंदगी जीने के लिए उम्मीद ही काफ़ी है । अब हर बदल बरसेगा , हर तारा चमकेगा , हर सपना पूरा होगा और हर ख़्वाहिश पूरी होगी ।

ख्वाहिशें अनकही

कुछ ख्वाहिशें है बोली , पूरी तो होगी । कुछ ख्वाहिशें है अनकही , कुछ अनसुनी , क़ाबू ना हो रही , पर सम्भालेंगे तब भी । उस डूबती हुई किरण व उगते हुए सूरज की उम्मीद , एक ख़्वाहिश चाँद को देखने कि bhi होती । उस सूखी हुई नदी के साथ बहते पानी की उम्मीद, एक वो भी ख़्वाहिश है अनकही । अब कहेंगे नही , पूरी करेंगे ख्वाहिशें , अब चलेंगे नही , दौड़ेंगे उन ख़्वाहिशों के लिए । पीछा करना है उन ख़्वाहिशों का , आगे बड़कर बदल जाए उम्मीदों में । एसी ज़िंदगी बितानी है जो इशारों पर नही , ख्वाहिशें पूरी करने में बीते । कुछ ख्वाहिशें है बोली , पूरी तो होगी ।

R.SusannaCelsia

Passionate writer, talented poet and creative blogger ,who has published a solo poetry book titled " Oasis of Poetry" . Who writes with a blend of fiction with reality

If .. My Brain Was A Tangible Place

If my brain were a tangible ,physical place ,it would be a vintage castle really really big one ,with a strong door with a board craved in metal saying" authorised thoughts only " .
The first chamber would a vintage office desk with papers and deadlines and work sheets ,a little messy and crowded ,which i try to arrange now and then and keep oragnised .
The second chamber is a beautiful magical heart shaped wall where polaroids of my favorite people are connected with fairy lights and neon stickers with notes regarding them imuze in this corner often.
Another part of this palace has a broken ,old golden framed mirror ,dusty with a diary with notes and pictures and markings ,this is a quite tough place for my thoughts ,cause its a part of reflection and correction. Then this beautiful garden of mine where hanging flowers and dhalias bloom ,a place where my thoughts rest and take flight where they see shooting stars and dreams. All my thoughts are happy staying here in this beautiful place.

If I Could Play The Violin

She ties her beautiful long hair ,
Walks to the meadows with her good friend,
The violin
She sits down in the lawn
And plays her dream instrument that mayhe lifeless but full
of life once her hand strikes the strings of the golden atique
violin
She plays and plays every notes my eyes dont see ,my ears
dont just hear but the vibrations could charge every particle
Feels like those notes are playing my red (chubby) harp ,my
heart
Feel like the notes have life and play my harp so loud
She plays and plays and plays and lavendars appear in the
green meadows and the yellow summer flowers fade away
And the purple clours appear in the evening .
She plays like her hands would never pain
She plays like its her solace
She plays like the every note meant a thousand words
She plays
In the sunset under the moonlight and the rain
She plays
If her notes can be stuck on golden parapus then it could be
the scripts ahead of you
Go on and read
The pain of melodies, that is the rythm of my hearts melodya
and the cry of the stabs in her heart ....
Go on

If I Could Heal Instantaneously

Sometimes its heard to understand what i really want or what i really need or what i even feel .
Because iv just got a label ,a label on my forehead, if you have only seen rubber stamps ,i call this molten wax stamps
I just returned from getting this stamp on my head as " failure "

Whatever i speak pr try to feel feels like a the groans of my deeply wounded heard
Or the painful melodies of a caged birdy
Sometimes melodies are too painfull too although they sound melodious to the ears if you search from the sheath it orginates ,it could be a torn heart moving back and forth and bleeding hands turning the heart into a harp

If i call failure as just a stamp someone gave me why does it actually matter souch ?
Why does it hurt ?
Can i just peel it off and walk my way
Can i just disqualify your tag and walk away ?
Maybe i can but my heart still remains as a torn sheath ,till you yourself remove that stamp
And all i choose to do it turn ruined sheaths into a harp
Lemme play till all camping around me sleep im peace as the melody soothes them and calms them
I choose not to groan but to gather my little hope and malkr use of my torn pieces

If Santa Had A Factory With Elfs

The little elf on Christmas eve

The world is so exiteted when the word Christmas i spelled .
The magic on my lips like gold sparkles from the elfs hat .
Imagine a barren cave so isolated and lonely,by the river that dried long ago
The old brach fallen of the tree lay there untouched as no creature walked by that way .
On a Christmas eve ,a little elf flung from santa's factory and fell over a hill tumbled and fell over a branch that broke and he mumbled and slid across a slopy hill and fell on a puddly lake that led him straight into a pool of fantasies that had a skating board he sat on the most different skate board and slid down the ice frozen lake
As the ice cracked he fell in the water entered his mouth and he chocked and he held a brach and moved out holding a ditry root of a wierd looking plant .
He flung up and landed in a land unkown
He looked left and right ,front and back .
Tried moving his arm and feet and all he heard was his own footsteps .
In happiness he jumped as he was out if his factory .
He had a chocolate cake in his pocket ,he gulped and slept all day
Till he got a letter from santa flying in the air with a beautiful paper with golden sparks .
He opned it with innocent look and found that santa was missing him
He threw away the letter and began exploring the barren land till he realized he felt really barren and lonley
And decided to go back to santa but there was no way for this
He sat down sat and frowning

Till he took of his cap in weary but found golden dust fall over the place and it turned into a place of warmth love ,belonged place full of happiness
"the spirit of christmas so warm and makes everyone feel belonged "
Christmas is all about God changing barren and sadness into being loved ,belonged and happy
He mumbled to himself as he wrote to santa back .
THE GIRL I WISH TO BE
all i strive to be is a girl there for you in the highest and lowest
I wish to smile and cry with you
I wish to walk with you in the meadows and dark valleys
I will never scold you or speak ill about you when your low
will always cry with u
And watch you rise up
In happy moments u can stand on yr own
But when your low i wish to hold your hands tight
And face it with you
When yr sad and lonley
I wont hurt you more asking you to become normal

If I Could Be Honest...

Those shoulders so bold taking all the pain ,taking all the burden ,those rough hands with a burden on their shoulders still with a smile wiping away our tears ,
Heart so soft that takes all my pain and absorbs it like a spong and doesn't revert any pain
Those rough hands that hold mine and take me along ,those rough lips that never complain and takes it all just to see their family smile
Those tough arms that protect those tough arms that make me feel like in a fotress
Those sharp eyes that see my pain through my heart and those eyes that i never saw tears in
Men are a blessing

If Only We All Understand This

So who is a sinner ,according to my standards, i can term anyone as a sinner ,and they can just dust it of their shoulders saying its not the same with my standards.

The word " fall short " means to miss the target ,so we all fall short of God' s standards ,and anyone who falls short of God's standards is a sinner ,so when we realize that we all fall into the same category called "sinners" we would stop criticizing, looking down on someone,and even forgiving someone is seen in a different perspective....

When we finally understand this we understand that we are all broken ,imperfect ,hurting people in need of a perfect God
,

The pharisees need God as much as the prostitutes and tax collectors ,because before God we are all imperfect in the same measure.

Wish The Society Realized Sooner

If you cant support her when she is alive and she's vulnerable to attacks then dont support her when she is dead and raped

If you stop judging her when shes alive and fine
If you stop pushing her away and blaming her when she asks for help ,you may not have to put angry stories after she is gone

When you are sexually harassed or assulteddont tolerate it and remm its not your mistake, and its the mistake of the harasser.

When she is so scared ,confused and traumatized, give her comfort ,support and justice
Please stop BLAMING HER!!!!

You don't deserve to be treated badly, dont stay quite when you are

You have all the rights to say NO !!! Dont hesitate to when you have to

Supriya U

Supriya was born in Bangalore. she has completed her MBA and now works in the banking sector. She loves reading books in her free time and the best moments of life are always with a book and cup of tea. She is an author of the book "Willing The Unwilling". She is also the Co-Author for two of the Anthology. And the proud mother of a princess.
Connect via
Instagram : https://www.instagram.com/supriya_udaykumar
facebook : https://www.facebook.com/supriya.priya.712

I Wish We Do Not Face Such A Situation Again!

Coronaviruses are a group of related RNA viruses that cause diseases in mammals and birds. In humans and birds, they cause respiratory tract infections that can range from mild to lethal. Mild illnesses in humans include some cases of the common cold (which is also caused by other viruses, predominantly rhinoviruses), while more lethal varieties can cause SARS, MERS, and COVID-19.

In cows and pigs, they cause diarrhea, while in mice they cause hepatitis and encephalomyelitis.

Coronaviruses constitute the subfamily Orthocoronavirinae, in the family Coronaviridae, order Nidovirales, and realm Riboviria. They have enveloped viruses with a positive-sense single-stranded RNA genome and a nucleocapsid of helical symmetry.

The genome size of coronaviruses ranges from approximately 26 to 32 kilobases, one of the largest among RNA viruses. They have characteristic club-shaped spikes that project from their surface, which in electron micrographs create an image reminiscent of the solar corona, from which their name derives.

So I formerly believe that I don't want any such viruses but a peaceful environment. So in this pandemic, many have suffered a lot, financially and non-financially. I could say even the globe wise we had a financial issue. Ok, let's keep the economy of the country aside and think about individually how each one has suffered in this pandemic. So there are people who faced depression, lost lives, lost family, missed family. What all we didn't face due to this pandemic. Ok, so the lockdown period was worst for some and comfortable for many.

I got to speak to many individuals directly, or through social media. So I'm going to share what/how people faced during the lockdown.

Life Of A Driver In The Pandemic

I got to speak to one of the cab driver. He was working with multiple travels. He was a 60 years old man. He has no help from his son. He has to take care of his earnings by himself. It was difficult for him to work, but he had no option other than to work. he had to earn, to live. He cannot strive or stay lazy because he has nobody to take care of him.

But he was earning sufficient to take care of him and his wife. It was then, it all started with the pandemic. He had no job like everybody. He stayed at home. He managed to supply sufficient necessities for his house. But how long did it last?. After April it was very difficult for him to manage with any money left with him. he burrowed with people. But he was not able to return. This created tension situation at home for him.

He was ready to do any work to manage the expenses at home.

His name is Kumar. He was working for OLA and also for other travels.

(the conversation on the phone was as below)

Hi Uncle- How are you? Hope you're enjoying staying at home.

Hi dear- I'm good! How about you? Enjoying ah? I'm struggling dear, without a job and money.

Yeah, uncle, I can understand. The situation is the same with all!

What to do dear. This pandemic is just subbing our life to a bigger extend

I managed to provide food for my wife, till now. Now I need to look for an alternative. I borrowed money from few people. All are forcing us to pay a higher rate of interest. A few more days, we will be without food too. I also need to pay for the electricity bill, water bill, and provisions.- he said with a worried voice

Uncle soon the pandemic will end and you can make it uncle. don't worry. I said with a low tone.

(He started to cry) I could hear them. But he hides them.

I said "uncle" with a low tone, my tone was just a reminder for him that he is talking to someone.

Oh sorry! Leave all that. I can handle it- he said after clearing his voice

I Wish We Do Not Face Such A Situation Again!

Post-pregnancy life in the pandemic.

This is something that I was waiting to tell the world, tell the world about my pregnancy and post-pregnancy story. In August 2019, I missed my monthly periods. Like all the married girls, I too was excited about the result. I decided to take the pregnancy test. I saw the two magical pink lines. I want to scream and tell the world about my pregnancy. But I want to make sure to tell everyone after it is medically confirmed.

I went to the urine pregnancy test. and waited till 2 pm for the results. But I didn't find them online. Hence I called the hospital directly and checked for it. The information or the result that she told us made me happy. Yeah finally medically it's now confirmed that " I'm pregnant"

I started to feel so happy. I just want to hug my husband and inform him that he is going to be a dad very soon.

I texted him in WhatsUp with all love emojis and informed him. Yeah, we are going to be parents very soon. Just a short period of 9 months. It was on 13th August, my dream came true. Nine-month pregnancy to fall in love for a lifetime.

So from August, my pregnancy days started with healthy food, positive thoughts, medicines, monthly checkup, the growth rate of the child, and whatnot. Everything that is included in the list of pregnant women.

So, till January everything was fine, but that's when we started to hear corona-virus. I call them the deadly virus. Might be there are more big or dangerous diseases. We had coronavirus rumors. When I turn towards the left, I could hear about this virus spreading in India too, and vice versa.

The government of India announces a lockdown. I mean complete lock-down, as u all know which means we cant go out of our homes. I was in my full-term pregnancy and was expecting my baby In this world anytime. Ok, let me tell you, the lockdown starts on Sunday and I had to visit a doctor on Monday, it was unavoidable. We left home for the hospital, and the hospital is just a min ride from home. I need not be worried about the virus, lockdown, or the police on the roads. I have a valid point to come out of the house.

We reached the hospital. and as per my doctor's advice, I was supposed to be get admitted to hospital on 26th March. And hospitals informed us, stating only one attendee with the patient. We had no clue what's going to wait for us in the hospital as this is our first child. Ok, so when we informed the same in the family, everyone suggested my husband stay with me. I agreed, in fact, happy with this decision. Because he had to take care of insurance also, so he had to be with me. any complication in delivery and the decision should be taken by him.

One attendee with a patient, I went into labor pain. My husband has no idea what has to be done. He was restless, he had no idea what's happening to me. all that he knows is I'm in labor pain. I was bleeding heavily, screaming. My mind was blind due to my pain. I could say, if somebody asks me if I take this pain again, they would reward me 1 crore, I would still say no.

After 4.5 hours of labor pain, I went into an emergency C-Section. We were blessed with a beautiful baby girl. Both the families welcomed us with a lot of love.

But the actual story started when we reached home. When our relatives wanted to see our kid.

Since the immunity is very low for the mother and the kid, the doctor said "DO NOT ENTERTAIN VISITORS" with all these restrictions, I and my husband decided that I would stay in my husband's place and would go to my mom's place sometime later after the pandemic.

my parents had to sit outside the house to see me and the kid. If a kid is sleeping, they had to wait outside the house. And sometimes we were forced to even closed the door, as after 4

pm uninvited guests "mosquitoes" are in huge. I used to feel bad for them. Insulting your parents in the name of a pandemic.

When they got a dress for the kid, we had to keep them outside leave them for 2-3 days, bring them inside, and put them directly into the washing machine. And immediately wash your hands.

Ok, so is my parents affected by coronavirus? Or the bag? Or the clothing that's inside the bag?

God! Do not give such a situation to any new moms. first thing, as a new mom I was into postpartum depression, lack of sleep. Tiredness, etc. on top of all this, something new I have to face.

Waiting for the good times!

(received this in an email from one of my cousins, when I told them I writing about people's experience in one of the anthology. I put myself into her shoes and felt the pain. Tired made its way.

Closing the door for parents is something we are forced to do because of pandemic or we are inhuman?)

I Wish We Do Not Face Such A Situation Again!

Life Of Person Working For One Of The Manufacturing Unit.

Hi, I want to share some of my experiences in this pandemic. I would like to introduce myself.

My name is Vinod. I'm been working for one of the manufacturing units for 28 years. My family consists of four people. My mom, wife, daughter, and myself My mother is around 70+

We are from Bangalore. My daughter has done her MBA and works for one of the corporate offices in Bangalore. when the pandemic started, my daughter started to work from the office. She started enjoying staying at home. Her life was busy on weekdays and free on weekends. During weekdays, she used to wake up by 9 am, freshen up, have her breakfast and start her work. and it goes till evening. She shut down her laptop and she was spending some time with us. She used to feel so good doing this for months.

But the case was not the same with me. initially, I was asked to work from home. Working in a machine is different, then laptops. Our work was just with machines. What have we got to do sitting at home in front of a laptop? We had 90% work in machine and 10% work in the laptop. And we had to do the machine work along with the laptop, that's how it works. At the same time, I was escaped from layoff too, because of my experience and career skills, and growth. Just thinking negatively! What if I had lost my job in this pandemic? It would have been a coffee without coffee powder. My life would have been plain hot water in the name of coffee.

And after few days we were asked to work as regularly, that's going to the office and work. I was worried. But I was helpless too!. However, It was on the first day of the office. I had an extra face mask, I don't know why did I have extra when I know one is sufficient. I had carried one small hand sanitizer. Next, it was already 6.30 am, my manager had communicated that we would start early than before, just to be on the safer side. "In a cab, there would be two employees and a driver" was the plan decided by the organization.

The cab arrived around 6.40 am and I saw one employee already. The driver checked my temperature, and he gave me a sanitizer. I sanitized my hands and then sat in the back seat of the car and there was space between two people.

We reached the office early than usual, as there was no traffic. Then we headed towards our office. Before entering the premises, we had a temperature check, again in the reception we had our temperature check. And then finally into my desk now. There was a distance between two employee desks

Our desk was too sanitized before we occupy them. What a situation we had to face. It was horrible. We can even enter our comfort zone freely.

Ok, fine let's ignore all this, my mind was not calm. I had my mother who is more than 70+. There was a rumour that we had to be careful of the people more than 60+ age as they will have less immunity. I was scared of this. This was hunting me a lot. But do I have an option?

After reaching home, I used to go to the washroom directly. Fresh up, make sure that I don't spread any virus, in case if I'm m affected. However to date, nobody is affected because of me, nor I was affected. My prayers are been answered always. My prayers are just to safeguard me and my family.

I WISH WE DO NOT FACE SUCH A SITUATION AGAIN!

ShilpaSahu

ShilpaSahu begin her story from a small town 'mauaima in allahabad.About writting, she is not a professional writer but one random day while scribbing on a piece of paper..she wrote something that was rhyming which seemed preetygood..It was the day when she realised how light it feels to pen down your feelings.

She feels that writing has provided her the liberty to portray her thoughts in today's eccentric world...She is writing since past one year and currently very fond of it.

She want to pursue a career in medical as she loves to help people by being doctor..She went off the home at a age of twelve in order to get the best education..She likes to gain knowledge from everything ..She always believe in being a normal human being and living her life to the fullest..

She loves her family the most especially her brother..

Her writing express her own experience and stories which most people can relate to...

Fb id- shilpa559@gmail.com

(1)

टूटा हुआ है हौसला ,
बुलंद हौसला करना है।

मुझे अपने सपनो को ,
हर हाल में पूरा करना है।

है जो सीने मे छोटी सी चिंगारी,
उसको शोला बनाना है।

मुझे अपने सपनो को ,
हर हाल में पूरा करना है।

बिगड़े हुए है हालात जो,
अब मुझे ना उसमे फसना है।

मुझे अपने सपनो को ,
हर हाल में पूरा करना है।

बचे हुए अब कुछ दिनों में ,
घनघोर परिश्रम करना है।

मुझे अपने सपनो को,
 हर हाल में पूरा करना है।

(2)

मुझे पढ़ना आता है,
मुझे लिखना आता है।

इस भीड़ भाड़ सी दुनिया में,
चमकना आता है।

मुझे चीखना आता है,
अपनी बात मनवाने के लिए।

मुझे लड़ना आता है,
अपने हक को पाने के लिए।

फिर क्यों डरू इस दुनिया से,
फिर क्यों झुकु इस दुनिया से।

मुझे आगे बढ़ते जाना है,
अपने शिखर को पाना है।

(3)

मैं अपने सफ़र में कई बार भटकी हूँ,
चलते चलते बेवजह सी बातों पर अटकी हूँ..

जिस राह भी चलती हूं
,सही लगने लगती है,
पर कुछ दूर जाकर मैं फिर पलटने लगती हूं..

मेहनत नहीं ,पर कहीं मन लगाना असल खेल है,
जो मन ना टिके कहीं, तो सारी मेहनत फेल है..

निराशा की आँधी ने कई बार मुझको तोड़ा है,
तिनके भर की आस से, मैनें हर बार खुदको जोड़ा है..

मेरी नाकाम कोशिशों का सिलसिला अभी जारी है,
क्योंकि सकारात्मकता से मेरी घनिष्ठ यारी है..

हाँ मैं हारी हज़ार बार हूँ ,एक जीत की तलाश में,
पर जो हार मान लूँ कभी तो समझना एक लाश में !

(4)

मेरी मंजिल बेहद करीब है.. वो सपना नहीं ख्वाब हैं वो ख्वाइश नहीं जिद हैं   ना जाने कितने अरसे से उसे सींचा हैं कितनी रातो ने उसे बुनते देखा हैं   आँसुओ के बाढ़ में भी वो बहा नहीं   घुसे की आग में भी वो जला नहीं   कई लोगो ने कोशिश की उसे मिटाने की पर वो कम्बख्त मिटा ही नहीं   भुला कैसे देते उसे वो सिर्फ सपना नहीं   ख्वाब हे जो हकीकत होने वाला हैं कुछ अरसे बाद पूरा होने वाला हैं   वो ख्वाब पहचान बनाने वाल हैं   वो ख्वाइश नहीं जिद हैं जो पूरा होने वाला हैं

(5)

तुम कहां हो? तुम्हें छोड़ आगे निकला है जमाना। तुम कहां हो? दुनिया जगमगाती हुई आगे बढ़ रही है.. क्यों तूने आंखें बंद, किसकी राह पुकारती हो। क्यों ऐसे मूक पड़े, दूसरों की सुन जाते हो। क्यों आसमा को एक टक, ऐसे तुम निहारते हो। समय आ गया है , समाज को दिखने का । समय आ गया है , कुछ अनोखा कर जाने का। फिर मत पछताना , यदि कुछ भी मत कर पाना। बस यही सोच लेना कि, आंखे आंधी थी , कान बहरे थे, परिजन तो कहते रह गए, खाली हम थक गए थे, समय दौड़ता गया , खाली हम थक गए थे। अब भी कुछ ना बिगड़ा है साथी, आखिर , तुम कहा हो?

Troyce Reimer

He was born in Belize Central America July 16, 1995, but at the age of 9, his family made the big move to Canada, where he has been living since. He is a friend to all he meets; his smile alone lights up a room as he walks in, and he absolutely loves meeting new people, he can talk to absolutely anyone, and he is an open book who loves to learn, connect and listening to people and hearing their life stories. He loves life, and loves all the people in it.

Where I Stand; The Man I Am; On My Land

I never give up on someone who's feeling gone, but when I feel like it, i'm left to deal alone, and said to be the toxic misfit, like if i'm just a stone, easy for them to quit, and stay out of my zone, because I am just a hypocrite, for feeling the pain to the bone, because they can't admit, the same pain they have also known, so they will rather threat to split, than to be someone grown, and make me out to be unfit, so I am overthrown, and I can't even aquit, or try to atone, just because they don't permit, and don't condone, and only omit, and stay over blown, instead of trying to submit, or loose the verbal tone, and instead of trying to knit the slit, of pain needing to be sewn, they take a drill bit, and go overblown, when I just want to remit, and go back to my throne, but then again I am hit, with the overtone, and reminded of being a misfit, and that I am prone, to never refit, without a grindstone, so I take the hit, bit by bit, till my split spirit, is gone with my wit, and I get spit, right on my grit, till you see my obit.

Now I've been shown, my capstone, that I am just a loan, easy to disown, always on postpone, worth nothing more than a groan, and made to dethrone, and apart i'm blown, like I am as brittle as freestone, and then unbeknown, but I do know, where I am homegrown, and I am a milestone, away, from the headstone, my grave, and I will not be a slave, to how I am expected to behave, its who I am worth thats worth to save, and I will be brave, and I will never cave, after everything I gave, I will conclave, and you will feel my shockwave, and I will never deprave, and I will engrave, and pave, my rave.

Its time for a new wave, after everything I forgave, time to be a threat like a heatwave, i'm the autoclave, hotter than a microwave, to any who misbehave, and my fury stave, those who want to enslave, the love I gave and save.. Anyone

unhappy to what I gave, is a architrave, you will mold away, while I enjoy the day, that I chose to walk away not to stay, and found my way, to find my own gateway, and I will not delay, or let myself decay, I will never stray, from my pathway, until I fade away, and reach my judgment day.. This is all I have to say, with this wordplay.. My enemies will not overstay, its doomsday, and I will slay, the rest will stay away at bay, and be nothing but a memory of yesterday, you better be a runaway, when I display my array, that my life is my broadway, I have no dismay, in who I display, because my Lords side is where I lay, and exactly where I am to stay.

Thinking About

I can't stop thinking about you, you took away my evening blue, giving my head a reminder clue, that you put a smile on my face, you're stuck in my head like glue, because you definitely are my ace, your love is what I wish I knew, you're someone I could never replace, especially when you take my mind to space, and not to complicate, but no more need to medicate, and this is not a race, no need to runaway or escape, this is real and this is the state, I feel for you like it is fate, and if that's a crime, then Ill just do the time, cuz this aint to mime, its a rhyme, and every line, comes without a thought of rhyme in mind, because you are my dime, so it just slides out of mind, silky and smooth like slime, I just wish you were mine, until the very end of time.

Out With The Old, In With The New;

You gotta let go of the old, to be open to the new, don't believe everything you're told, because it's not always true, don't wait till you're old, to learn what you already knew, just gotta be bold, and don't let them see you like a menu, cuz a real heart is never cold, its really hotter than you, and when together you mold, there's nothing you cannot do, and your love could never be sold, cuz all they will want is you, and you'll have what you want too, and you will be bound together like glue, and it all starts with a "I want you", and a "I want you too", and then together you will never be two, because you will share a same love, that is true, having something long over-due, and you will finally get the clue, that you will never again wonder who, you should pursue, because you finally withdrew, from the people you outgrew, and decided to renew, after everything the two of you, on your own have been through, now you're able to subdue, and now you both got your queue, that you fit together like the pair to a shoe, and it's time your love really flew, and brew together like stew, in ways no one could ever outdo, because you have me, and I have you.

Knock, Knock

You really do amaze me, which makes me happy as can be, and it may be, why my heart is racing, and my smile is gaping, if only you were mine for the taking. You make my soul sing, made my spirit king, and now my eyes are watching, letting me see, what we could be, revealing the mystery, that they call destiny. And now these commotions, have turned my emotions, from motionless, to full explosions. And now feelings have rushed, and my doubts have been crushed, so that negativity could be brushed. For me to be able to say, every single day, that im here to stay, so everything we ask and pray, will finally go our way, so we can live today, and every other day, as we may, without running away, so we can display, and portray, our hooray, without delay. So I hope you understand, where I stand, as a man, searching for a plan, to have a future, without another detour. To have something to live for, that is much more, than we've ever had before, and have much more to adore. With endless variety to explore. That's why I'm knocking at your door.

Dreamer, Or Doer?

I am a dreamer, I am a lover, I dream about love, and I love to dream, I find myself dreaming through out my days, which is not as good as it may seem, because when you want a dream to come true, it can put a hole in you, and it can be for no reason, taking you out like a black ops team, so trained and silent, taking you out so quiet and viciously, as if you committed treason. But you keep dreaming so carelessly, when you want something to be real, if you keep on dreaming it's like, speaking to the devil and signing a deal... Now the reason for this is, some dreams are too good to be true, but you always, just gotta do you, if you want something so bad, don't let the dream take you out, prove what you are all about, if you want to be the number one dad, go out there and prove you are, and trust me, you will never be sad, if you want something, go and get it, if its too far out of your grasp, quit it before you regret it, keep on dreaming and it will eat you out, it will stick to your mind while you're out and about, see your dream for what it is, and you will see clearly again, and the rest of your life will be a gain, so you can be happy and make it remain, love yourself and don't dream the impossible, do what is you and make your happiness possible. Yes i am a dreamer, and every day makes me meaner, I just keep getting so eager, But that is because I dream for love, and love is something you cannot control, I guess you can say it comes from up above, oh but it's so beautiful, like a glowing white dove, just staring at you, until you have found it, so you can spread your own wings, and so you can be bounded, with those rings, but it's okay to dream a bit, dreams keep us going, if we dont let it get to big, because the future is unknowing, but do not stop believing, just dream something that leaves no grieving. Its gotta be something that's possible, so your mind is not stuck in the impossible. Don't get me wrong, almost anything is possible, when you

have a plan to plot, but some things are not, don't let it go on for too long, don't let the dream be all you've got. Are you a dreamer or are you a doer? Wish i knew sooner.

Love

Some people say, loving someone is a sickness. That statement is true, although loving someone is a sickness, them loving you too, is the healing potion. When two people are in love, nothing will get in their way, not one single thing in this whole world can come between love. In sickness and in health, love, love will always be there. In life or in death, love, love will always remain. When you love someone, truly love someone, although you may "move on", your heart will never forget that special person. Does not matter what happens, "moving on" never actually means that you lost love for someone, all that means, is that you are trying something new. No thing, nor no one, can ever replace that love. Love is forever. I believe, love is the most powerful existence known to man kind, nothing will ever over rule love, Love can be bitter, love can be sweet, but without it, we are nothing, nothing will ever replace love. Nothing

UMME HANI

Umme Hani is a 16 year old girl. She is fond of reading and writing since 2 years,believes in herself and also believes that self love is most important thing in life,she is a positive girl with a positive thoughts.

Glimpse Of Love ....

I always wish for you.
When I'm lonely,I always think of you.

When you are lonely I wish you love.
When you are awake,I wish you success.

When things are complicated.
I wish you a peaceful mind.

When you are in trouble.
I wish you a strength.

When you are depressed.
I wish you a bliss.

When you are agreed.
I wish you satisfaction.

Do you believe in love?
If yes, then you wish to have that person.
You can't touch love,
You can't see love,
But you can feel it.

Once I closed my eyes,
I only felt your voice,
Though you weren't there,
But I can feel your voice.

Like a flower with no fragrance,
This is how I will be without you,
I wish to have you,
Always forever.

Then I Made A Wish A Wish For Love...

I still remember that time when I was small and standing with my mom and peacefully I was looking at the sky.then suddenly I saw a glittery line falling and I asked my mother what is it then my mother said it is a shooting star and our grand parents says after seeing the shooting star whatever wish you make will come true

now after 15 years I'm helpless, I'm broken,I love him but I can't marry him. because he is from another caste.

Why this happens in our country everyone should have rights to live freely, peacefully.if they go against their family their family doesn't accept them

And social pressure make life stressful for the couple survival becomes different for the couple financial issues are faced by the couple and they have to listen taunts regularly

People strongly prefer to marry their children in the same caste or religion if someone oppose it and falls in love,with the person of different caste and religion then they have to fight against their family.....inter religion caste marriage faces different problems in few cases it is very difficult for them to fight for their love and in some cases it is very easy parents are very calm and calmly they accept the decision of their children

A girl who is in love with the guy of another caste and is fighting for his love...I was not allowed to go anywhere and I was limited to home and collage.when I met him, he made me realise the meaning of life..we wanted to marry each other but our parents refused our proposal and at the end .I was forced to get married.

I was standing under the sky wearing my wedding clothes with heavy jwellery and I saw a shooting star and remembered once my mom told me about the shooting star and then I made a wish, wishes I want and with the god grace got married to my man.

NEER PATEL

Neer Patel is a actuarial student living in the lights of Mumbai . He is providing his lines independently on @neerpatel11. He is a ghost writer since his late teen age . He writes in english and hindi his writing consist of short poems , couplets , short story and poems . he can be connected with neerp.2002@gmail.com .

(1)

मुझसे मिलने आओ, तो फुरसत से मिलने आना,
लम्हों की किश्तों में तुम्हें देखना मुझे गंवारा नहीं ।

वक़्त बचा लेना, खदु का श्रृंगार मत करना तमु ,
वो मोहब्बत की क्या , जिसमें मैंने तुम्हें संवारा नहीं ।

यू तो सफ़र में हमसाथी बन चलने को कारवां है,
पर राहे हयात में, मंजूर हमें दूजा कोई सहारा नहीं ।

तेरे गालो के तिल पे, अटका हुआ मेरा दिल है
जो धड़के सीने मेरे में, दिल तुम्हारा है हमारा नहीं ।

जिसकी मदभरी मुस्कान से रोशन है महफ़िलें,
कैसे कह दू की उस बला पे पत्थर दिल हारा नहीं ।

चल आओ मुझे मकुम्मल करने जिदंगी में मेरी,
सपनो में होती मुलाकात से मेरा होता गुजारा नहीं ।

मोहब्बत में यार की, सच्ची इबादत सीख ली मैंने,
खदुा बना दया उसे और फिर कभी उसे पुकारा नहीं

(2)

खुद को मैं अब हर जगह ढूढता हूं
जीने की बस एक वजह ढूढता हूं

न धरती पर मि ली न अंबर पे
अपने लि ए एक सतह ढूढता हूं

हआु करते थे कभी मेरे ख्वाब अब मंज़ि ल,
और की तरह ढूढता हूं

यूंही वक्त-ए-हयात गुज़र गया
अब क्यों मौसम बेवजह ढूढता हूं

Hope U Remember The Night

It was a night of the moon
you remember the night i was with you
When we crashed into eachother's lives
On the bridge that connected us two
I had lived long, away from all
You were the one, and only to come
When i was at the edge all alone
I remember yours, it was
Chaos You were sarching, for the sea to come
You were tired of time, and wanted the stream to stop
You were my call for life to come
And i were your sea of love
We both had promised
To be together for all
Do you remember that night
Those constalations had audienced
That night we crashed into lives of one another
Do you remember the days you were loved

(4)

In the world of harsh noice, And painful screams, I found peace in you, Like in fresh water streams, Like when the wind blows, Touching face. Like the end rope, In a hurdle race. Like beautiful flowers, In the mid spring. Like the soft feathers, In bird's wing. Like clouds, In a sunny day. Like the sun, When winters stay. In the world of harsh noice, And painful screams. I found peace in you, Like in fresh water streams.

(5)

My 1 AM There is something peaceful about 1am It's past the hustle of midnight It's before the sleep deprivation at 2am It's right in the middle of not knowing what to do And feeling there are too many things to do There's something hopeful about 1 am The memory of a day spent well sinks in The assurance of a day well begun seeps out It's a feeling of a day, right in the middle of night There's something about 1am, alright!

(6)

Only u stay It is only you who stays, Borrowed light from the sun. On a full moon I am at craze, Always unexpectedly into you I run. Leaving on certain days, My eyes search for you. This love for you with all the praise, My longing heart, you always knew. All these spots on your beautiful face, Does not matter my love. To the ends of time I will chase, Me on earth; you watch me from above. No one sees me, But the silver moon!!

(7)

I sit wrinkled on a broken chair With none around for vibes to share The walls are inching closer by each day As if wanting to crush me into the air The pillow is drenched from tears I weep On raw evenings possess no blankets to keep Shivering and Starving, days almost pass Only photographs I find to revive the past I crave for light, for a partner on the other side For screams and laugh, a sight of life But reduced to torn clothes, frozen bones and skin which is pale It feels dreadful and I am looking for a bail My chest feels heavy, body so paralyzed The pain spreads evenly, this is the end I realize But it doesn't kill leaving me still jailed Yet Again, I wake up struggling the unfair as I sit wrinkled on a broken chair.

(8)

Some day Some days I wanna disappear Some days I wish I didn't fear deep waters so much that I could drown And some days I just wanna be found... Some days I wanna run away Some days I wanna lose my way And end up buried under the ground And some days I just wanna stick around... One day I hope I never look behind One day I hope I lose my mind Make a fool of myself, become a clown And one day I hope I wear a crown

Flairs and Glairs, a platform by a student for the students. We are esteemed youth struggling to carve out our path for our future and we follow a basic mindset Since everyone is not born with all-round skills. Joining hands with people who are born to execute it with perfection is the best way to evolve. Self-Evolution is the need of the hour but, evolving as a community is what we strive for. The initiative as kickstarted by, Founder- Mr. Shubham Shah with the motive to utilize the skillset and talent of writing has now a team of 10+ people who are actively participating into newer forms of learning and discovering talents among youngsters. We Provide platform and services like Publishing opportunities, Open mics, Workshops, Hands-on training. Operating with Brand Name of Flairs and Glairs (Publication House), we offer the chance of elevating a passionate writer to an esteemed author With Brand name Teekhe Zasbaaat. We bring to you an opportunity to get accustomed with the Public Speaking and Presenting of Thoughts along with regular challenges to brush up your inking spirit. The newest initiative to extend our services we introduced in a new writing Platform- The Glittering Fables and Ink Over Tears.

We Choose to Fly Like A Falcon than to be

a Leg Pulling Crab.

To Know More: Infoline – 7781900870
Mail Us At-
flairsandglairs@gmail.com / info@flairsandglairs.in
Or Visit is at
www.flairsandglairs.com / www.flairsandglairs.in
Social Handles- @flairsandglairs @teekhezasbaaat